Love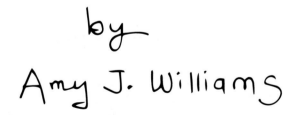

catches up

with

Wanda Petunia

by

Amy J. Williams

Balboa Press books may be ordered through booksellers or by contacting:

Balboa Press
A Division of Hay House
1663 Liberty Drive
Bloomington, IN 47403
www.balboapress.com
1 (877) 407-4847

ISBN: 978-1-4525-1713-1 (sc)
ISBN: 978-1-4525-1714-8 (e)

Printed in the United States of America.

Balboa Press rev. date: 11/06/2014

BALBOA.
PRESS
A DIVISION OF HAY HOUSE

She was in Love with a wonderful man.

He said he loved her too.

"WANDA, I love you to the ends of the EARTH!"

...until she found

him

in the arms of another.

years

wonds's

She
believed
him ...

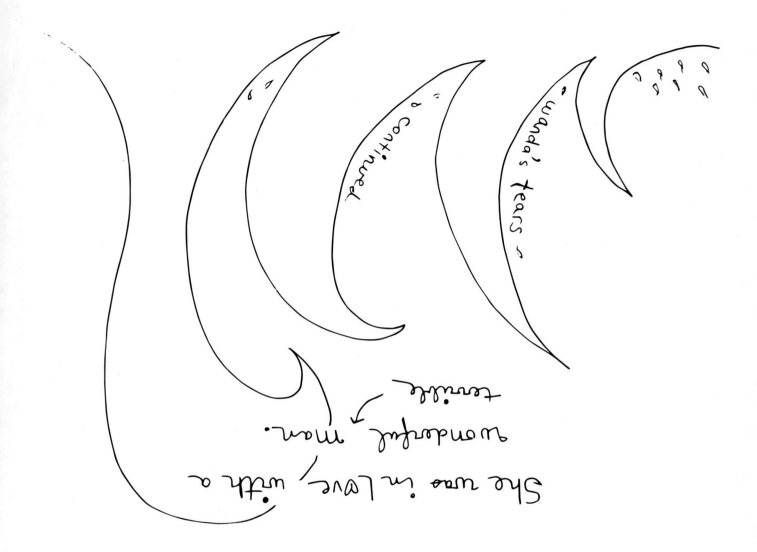

She was in love with a wonderful man.

terrible

continued

Wanda's tears

Unfortunately for
Wanda Petunia,
she had just
come home
from Sunday School.

While there, her teacher
read the
verse:

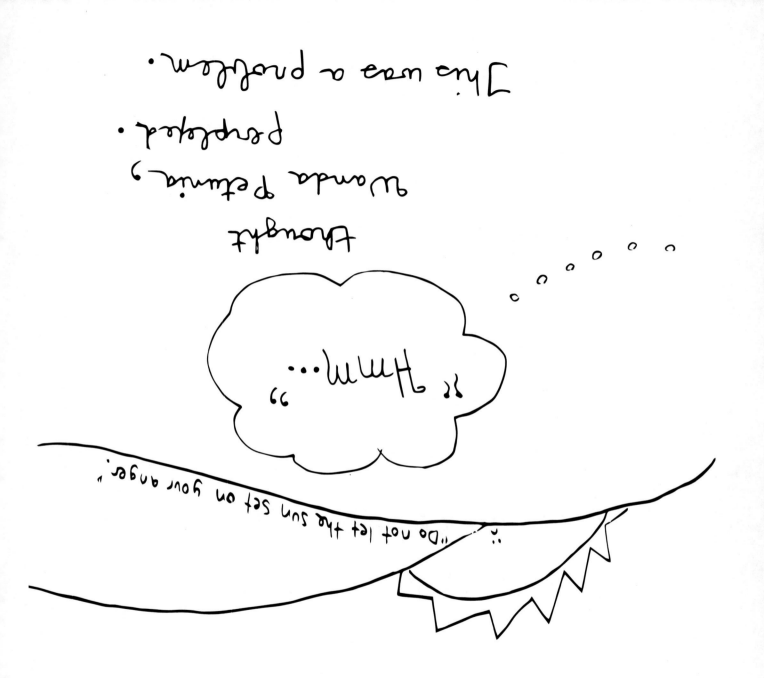

Wanda Petunia
was
no stranger
to
problems.

She had to figure out
which shoes to wear.

Orange matte

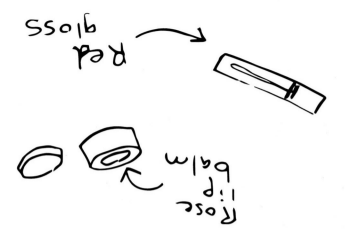

Red gloss

Rose lip balm

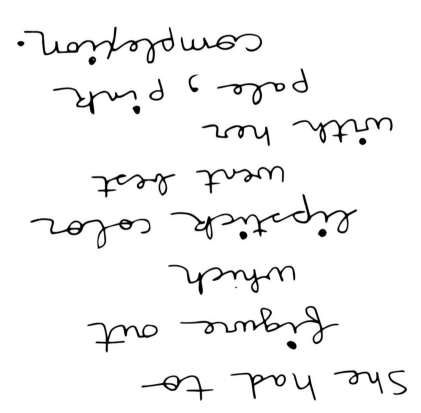

She had to figure out which lipstick color went best with her pale, pink complexion.

BUT this was new territory for ☞ Wanda Petunia

HOW could she keep the sun from setting on her anger?

ready to move on.

Not

Wanda Petunia
Was

Wanda Petunia
knew
She just got got?

She asked her neighbor
to
feed her cat,

She gassed up
her convertible,
and

She hit the road!

It had been
early in the day
when
Wanda Petunia
saw her
beloved
in a liplock
with an old
sow.

wanda's

tears

continued

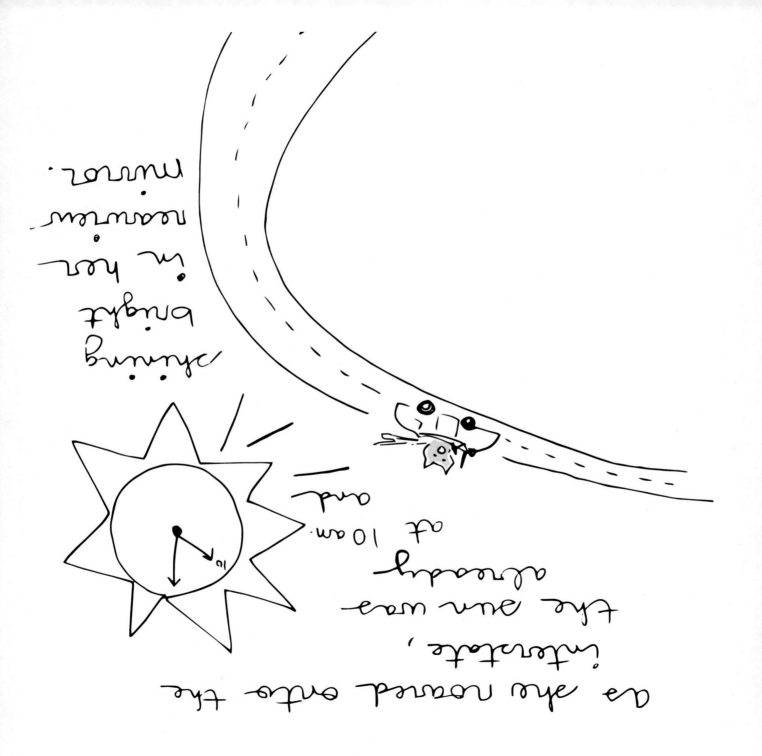

The bright morning haze turned into a more intense midday glare, and by late evening she was losing her lead.

But, she knew it was getting **DARKER.**

Somewhere in the Mid-West, the sun was setting...
on her anger.

Even though the day's end was in sight,
there was no end in sight for her anger.

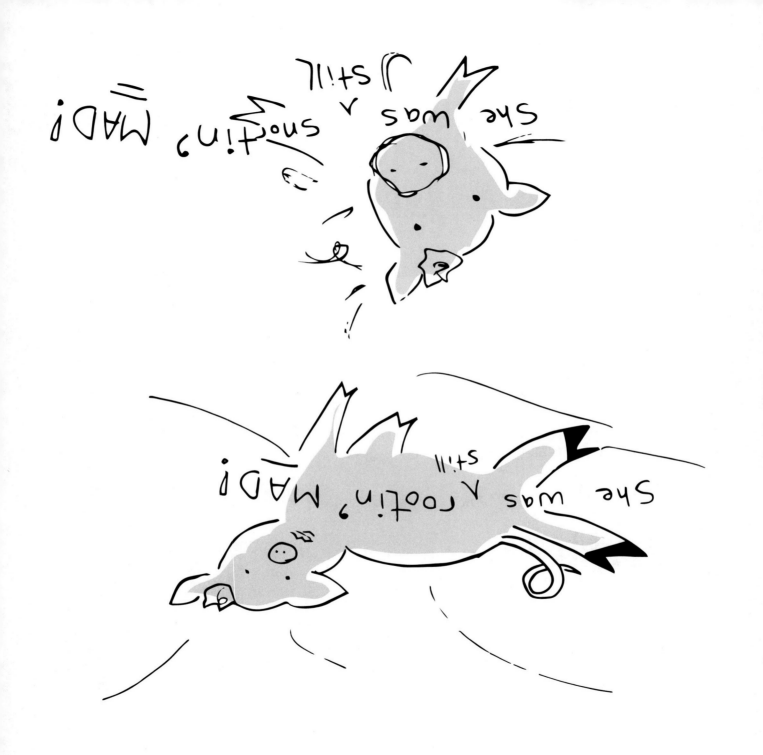

But Wanda was also tired.

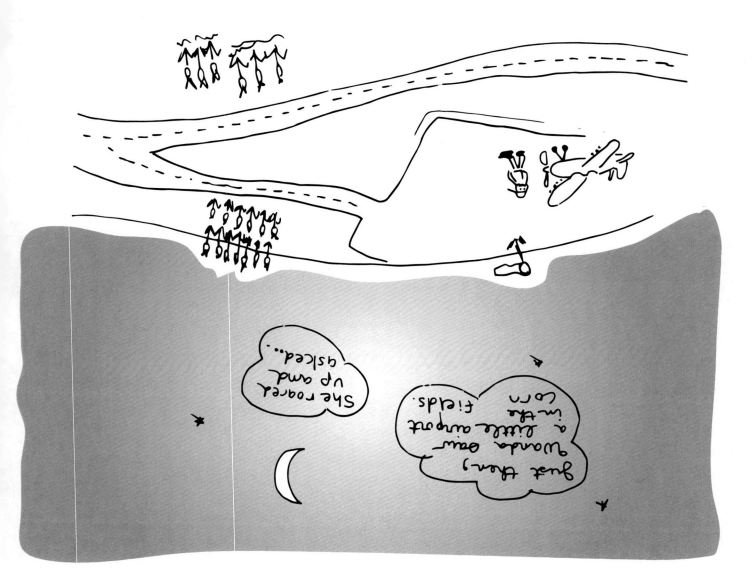

a crop dusting pilot agreed, and Wanda climbed into his plane.

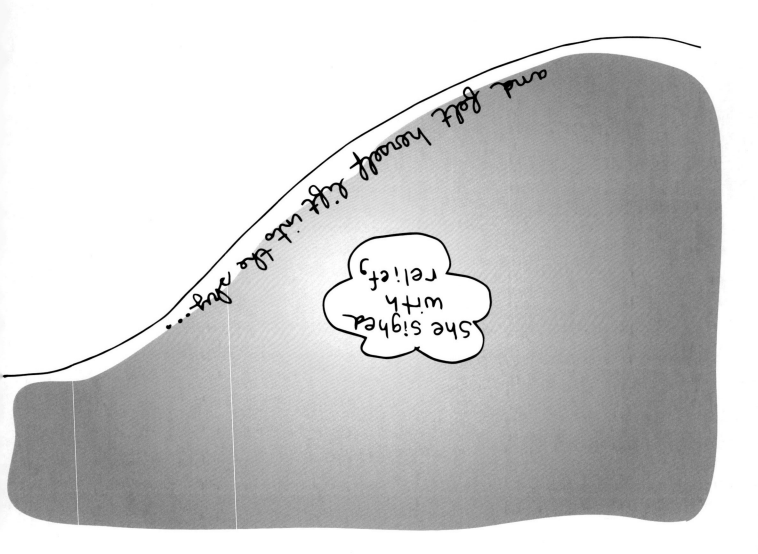

Wanda Petunia looked down at the corn fields...

and back at the sun.

It was hot on
her pig tailes.

With ANGER burning in her heart, could she beat the setting sun ?

Wanda Petunia was travelling with the sun, but it was faster. It was dusk when the plane Wanda commandeered...

HOLLYWOOD

saw the Hollywood sign.

When the plane landed
at L.A.X., it
caused quite a commotion.

But, Wanda was
on a
mission.

RUSHING TO THE TICKET COUNTER,

Wanda Petunia pulled out her credit card and passport

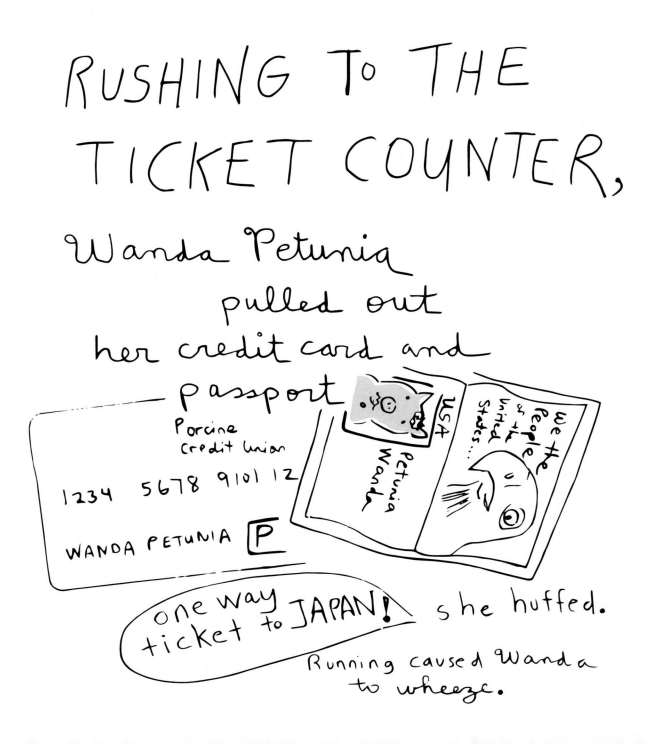

Porcine Credit Union

1234 5678 9101 12

WANDA PETUNIA [P]

USA
Petunia
Wanda

We the People of the United States...

"one way ticket to JAPAN!" she huffed.

Running caused Wanda to wheeze.

When there was
a hint of
midnight left,
Monday jumped
jet took off.

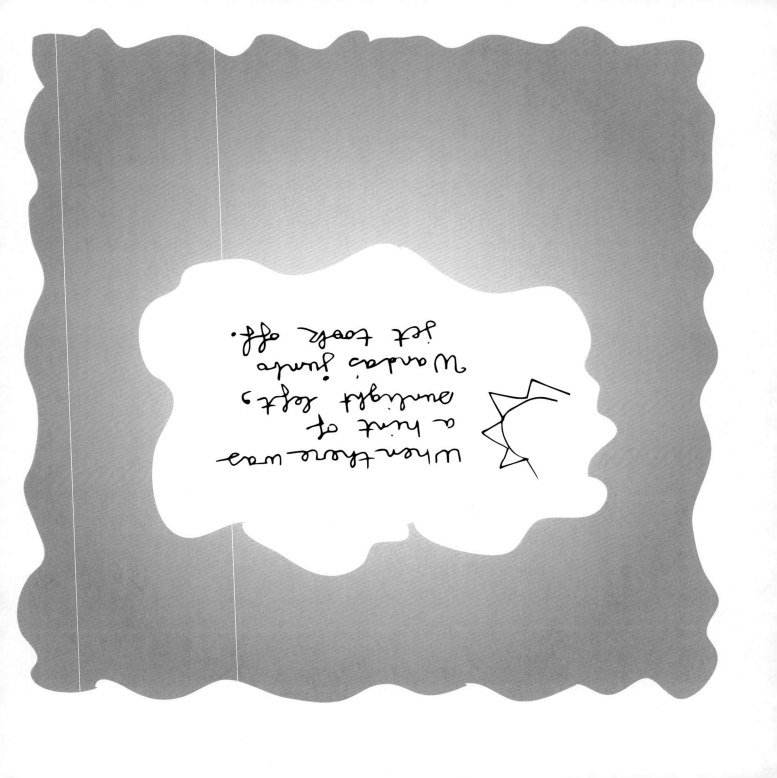

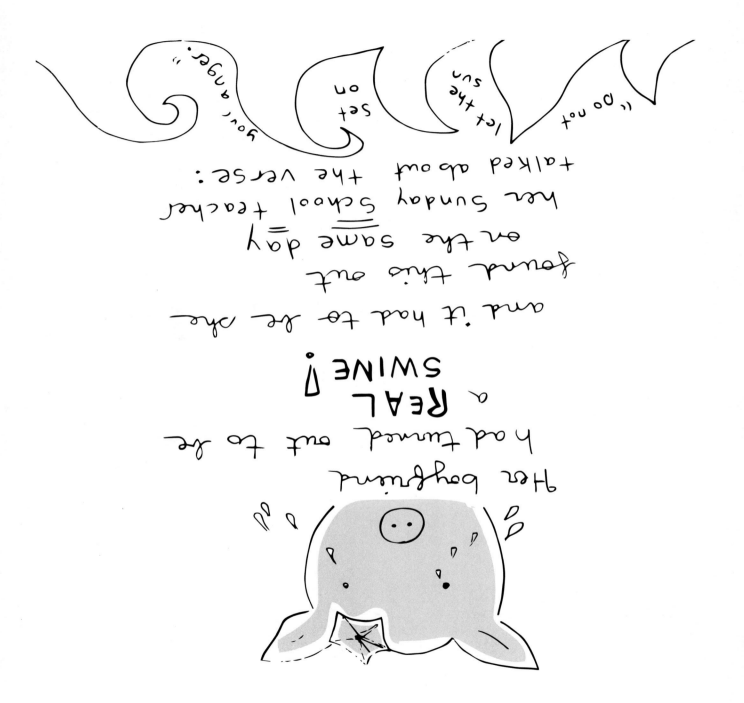

Her boyfriend had turned out to be a REAL SWINE!

and it had to be she found this out on the same day her Sunday School teacher talked about the verse:

"Do not let the sun set on your anger."

With relief,
Wanda noticed
her plane
was catching
up with
the sun.

She had hope.

Wanda loved Japanese style.

She wanted to stay and shop, but the sun was hot on her pig tail again.

after landing in Japan, with the sun in the afternoon sky, she got her next flight to **india**

Wanda loved Indian curry. She even had a pierced nose.

But the sun kept advancing on Wanda's HOT, SPICY ANGER.

HRMPH! she grumbled.

Just escaping
another setting
sun,
Wanda headed
to the worst place
in the world for
a pig with a
broken heart 😢😢:
FRANCE.

Narrowly escaping the sun's setting
it was evening
when
Wanda Petunia
landed
in
FRANCE ... in Paris.

Truffles.

She decided to hunt for

Wanda did the only thing she could think of...

Wanda headed to the ONLY place a respectable person would do: the ruffle shop.

At the shop, "Ye Olde Truffle Shoppe," Wanda saw a TALL **BEEFY** Parisian pig behind the counter.

Wanda Petunia's
heart
melted...

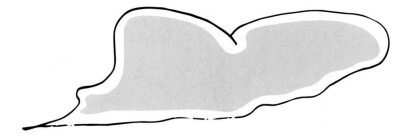

...so did her anger...

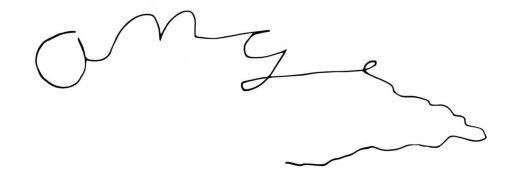

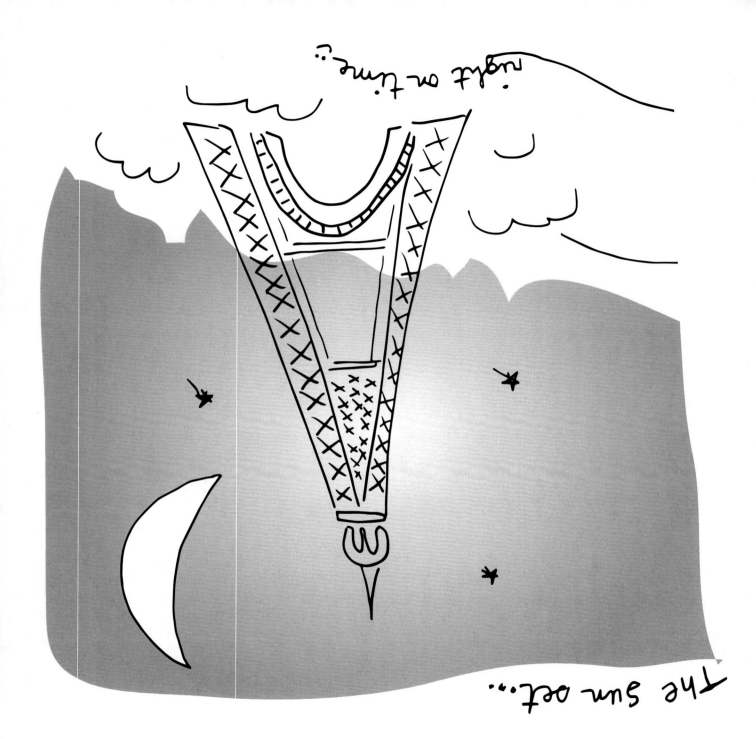

Follow
Wanda's
adventures:

http://amywilliamswellness.com/
wanda-Petunia/

Layout:
markwolfedesign.com
oink ☺

As a teen, Amy Williams was fired from her first job when she complained that the sprinklers on a pig farm were turned off on a hot, summer day. Pigs don't sweat and needed the water to stay cool. Wanda Petunia was born from Amy's care of other beings and hopes Wanda Petunia will help you learn to love all beings, including self!

Printed in the United States
By Bookmasters